Mystery Baby:
A Jolimichel Production
THE GLASS TEA POT

WRITTEN BY JOLIMICHEL ROBINSON
ILLUSTRATED BY RON CUNNINGHAM

AuthorHouse™
1663 Liberty Drive
Bloomington, IN 47403
www.authorhouse.com
Phone: 1 (800) 839-8640

Published by AuthorHouse 01/31/2018

ISBN: 978-1-5462-2595-9 (sc)
ISBN: 978-1-5462-2596-6 (e)

Library of Congress Control Number: 2018901115

Print information available on the last page.

Any people depicted in stock imagery provided by Thinkstock are models,
and such images are being used for illustrative purposes only.
Certain stock imagery © Thinkstock.

This book is printed on acid-free paper.

authorHOUSE®

DISCLAIMER

All names and characters mentioned and/or illustrated in Mystery Baby: A Jolimichel Production, The Glass Tea Pot, are purely fictitious and do not resemble any known characters. All characters appearing in this work are fictitious. Any resemblance to real places, and/or persons, living or dead, is purely coincidental.

Misty is on the phone with Nancia.

Misty: Yes Nancia, I am looking forward to going shopping with you today! But you know my cousin Bran Lee is in town.

Nancia: How long will she be staying with you?

Misty: Well since she just got hired at the Weathertons residence, she'll be staying with me until she can get the rest of her things moved in over there.

Nancia: Is she going shopping with us?

Misty: No, I have to drop her off at the Weathertons and then we can go shopping from there!

Misty, Nancia, and Bran Lee are in the car.

Misty backs into the driveway of the wealthy Weathertons house, and hears a loud "crunch" under her wheels.

The three women get out of the car and run to the back of the trunk.

They notice a simple set of dishes broken under the tire: a plate, saucer, cup, and teapot.

Misty: Oh no!

Bran Lee: You ran over Mrs. Weathertons dishes?

Nancia: The teapot did not break. It's still intact!

Misty investigates the dishes. Nancia reviews the teapot.

Misty: I'm going to have to replace these dishes.

Bran Lee: A single place setting is $250.00!

Nancia: Why is there only one place setting?

Misty: $250.00 for a single place setting?

Bran Lee: At least the teapot did not crack.

Nancia: Look what's inside the teapot?

All three women are staring into the teapot.

Misty: It's a key!

Nancia: I wonder what it unlocks?

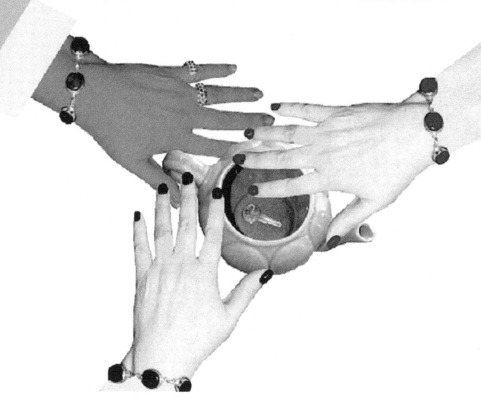

Bran Lee: I don't know but we need to replace it—we need to replace the dishes and return the key. But I have no clue where to buy a replacement, or even if one is available. I cannot lose this job over a simple set of dishes!

Misty: You won't, we will find a replacement set. I will look on the internet. With a price like that, it has to be somewhere!

Bran Lee: Come on, stop kidding, this is serious. I need to replace this set of dishes, now.

Misty: Ok, I will check the internet and contact Johnny for more help. You check inside the Weatherton's house for any signs of where these dishes might have come from.

Nancia: I will check out some of the expensive sets of dishes in town at The Jolly Merchant store.

Misty: Come on Nancia, let's go shopping.

Bran Lee: Bye girls, have fun. I will see you later.

Meanwhile, Misty and Nancia drive off to shop at the Jolly Merchant.

Nancia: How are we going to return the key?

Misty: We can't return it until we have both the dishes and the key, together.

Nancia: But what if we can't find a replica of those dishes, and Mrs. Weatherton needs the key beforehand.

Misty: Well... that would depend on what the key is for.

Nancia: How can we know?

Misty: A locksmith would know. But let's see if we can find that set of dishes—then we won't have to worry about the key!

Misty and Nancia walk down the aisles of the JOLLY MERCHANT.

Nancia: We're not finding anything!

Misty: Let's go to the cashier at the counter and see if she can help us.

Cashier and Roger (her cash-register computer) stand at the counter.

Misty: Hello, maybe you can help us! We have accidently broken an expensive set of dishes and we would like to replace it. We were wondering if you carried anything like that.

Cashier: (looks at Roger) I know that we do carry items like that. Roger, would you be able to tell us where something like that would be?

Roger brings up pictures of different dish settings.

Misty looks at the pictures and identifies the set of dishes that the girls are searching for.)

Misty: Yes! That set is the one we need!

Roger (says on his screen): We're sorry, but that one is out of stock! It can be ordered, but it will take two days to receive.

Nancia: Two days?

Misty: Oh dear! Well... we must order it!

Cashier: Alright then! All we need is some information so that we can know whom to contact when the set comes in.

Misty and Nancia give Cashier and Roger the information.

As they leave the store, they realize that the key is still an issue.

Nancia: Now what are we going to do about the key, until the dishes come in?

Misty: Well first of all, we need to know how urgent the key is to Mrs. Weatherton. We will need to contact a lock smith so that he can tell us what the key would unlock. If it is a key to her front door, she most likely has another one and may not need to find this one just yet.

Nancia: And if it belongs to something else?

Misty: Then I guess we'll have to cross that bridge when we come to it! But if it turns out to be a key that she needs to have back today, then we will have to tell her that her dishes are broken and we are still waiting for them to come in.

Misty goes home to her town house. She picks up the telephone and calls Johnny.

Johnny: Hello?

Misty: Hello Johnny! I have an incident that needs your help!

Johnny: What's going on?

Misty: Well, Nancia and I stumbled upon a key that we need to have identified.

Johnny: A key?

Misty: Yes! Well, as you know, Bran Lee was staying with me, and she was recently hired by the Weathertons to be their live-in house keeper! But when Nancia and I dropped her off at their house, we accidently ran over a box of dishes that was sitting in front of their garage! The tea pot did not break, but the others did. So now, Nancia and I are trying to replace the dishes.

Johnny: So what about the key?

Misty: Well, a mysterious key was sitting inside the tea pot! We don't want to let Mrs. Weatherton know this until we can replace the dishes! So we were wondering if you could recommend a locksmith who could identify the key. We need to know how urgent giving it back to her would be.

Johnny: Yes, Binford has a friend who is a lock smith. Let me get with him and see if he can identify the key!

Johnny and Binford research LockBear from Binfords office.

Binford: Yes John! According to the computer, LockBear is still at the same address. Let's have the girls meet us at his office and see if he can identify the key for us.

Misty, Nancia, Johnny, and Binford are standing in LockBear's office.

LockBear: (examines the key) Yes, I believe I know what this key would open.

Johnny: Yes?

LockBear: This is a key for a safety deposit box over at Jolly Town Bank!

Johnny, Binford and the girls look over at each other.

Johnny: Thank you LockBear! Thank you so much for your help!

Johnny, Binford and the girls stand at the car.

Johnny: (toward Misty and Nancia) Surely you are going to tell Mrs. Weatherton that you found this key, aren't you?

Misty: Johnny, if we tell her about the key, then we have to reveal that we broke her dishes!

Nancia: And if we expose the broken dishes before we replace them, then Bran Lee may lose her job!

Binford: I can't believe that Mrs. Weatherton would end Bran Lee's job over a mistake!

Misty: We don't want to take that chance!

Johnny: Well....I have an idea....but it sounds crazy, even to me!!

All: What is it?

Johnny: Let's go over to the bank and have the bank teller look inside the safety deposit box. Without revealing to us what is in there, she could help us know how urgent the key is to Mrs. Weatherton.

Binford: You must be kidding, man! That idea is crazy!

Misty: But if it's just an old keep sake, she may not notice the key missing.

Nancia: Then we would have time for the new dishes to come in, and we could return everything together!

Misty: We don't even have to return it! We could just leave everything in the corner of the garage as it was before.

Johnny, Misty, Binford, and Nancia drive over to Jolly Town Bank.

The Bank teller examines the key and takes them to the bank deposit box.

All of them look together.

All: It's a letter!

Nancia: Well Mrs. Weatherton might not need this key immediately, if the only thing she has locked in this safe deposit box is a letter!

Misty: (Reads the letter aloud)

Dear Wilma,

On the sale of the beautiful house that you and your dear, Wilbur has moved into—I just want you to know about the "secret" room, located behind the west wall of the basement.

This room is located behind the book case, up against the wall. The button to activate the revolving wall is behind the Encyclopedia book with the emblem of the letter "D". D is

for door, of course.

They close up the safe deposit box.

Misty: Mrs. Weatherton must have kept this letter, and it is very special to her—she's locked it away.

Johnny : Well the most important thing to do now, is to replace the dishes, restore the key to the glass tea pot, and forget this event ever happened.

Misty: (Ponders) Yes...but I wonder what is behind the door of the secret room.

Nancia: Perhaps it's simply for storage!

Johnny: Well, in any case, it will be good for Bran Lee to know that another room exists in the house.

Misty: Yes, I will let her know so that she won't accidently dust the wrong book on the book case!

Binford: And in the meantime, we will need to replace those dishes, and restore this key to the glass tea pot! Johnny, Binford, Nancia, and Misty all leave the bank.

Misty is alone at home in her bedroom, talking to Bran Lee on the telephone.

Misty: Does Mrs. Weatherton know that we ran over the box of dishes in the drive way and broke them?

Bran Lee: No, I don't even know if she knows that the dishes were there.

Misty: Well good! The new dishes should be in by tomorrow. But what I wanted to tell you is that we did discover the identity of the key, and the safe deposit box that it unlocks at Jolly Town Bank!

Bran Lee: Oh, how exciting!

Misty: Well, apparently, Mrs. Weatherton had a private letter locked away in the safe deposit box!

Bran Lee: (in a reprimanding voice) Misty! You presumptuously read a private letter in Mrs. Weatherton's safe deposit box?

Misty: We weren't being presumptuous, Bran Lee—we needed to know how important the key was to Mrs. Weatherton, and if she would need the key, located in the box of broken dishes, before we would be able to replace the dishes!

Bran Lee: Oh...

Misty: Anyway, it turns out that she would not immediately miss the key. However, an old letter was in the safe deposit box, and the bank teller allowed us to read it.

Bran Lee: What did it say?

Misty: It says that there is a secret room in the house that you will be staying in.

Bran Lee: A secret room?

Misty: Apparently, there is a book case in the west wall of the basement. Behind the encyclopedia book initialed with the letter "D". You will need to be especially careful when you dust that book case.

Bran Lee: Yes! I certainly will! Thank you for telling me about this.

Misty: I will let you know when THE JOLLY MERCHANT calls us about the dishes!

Bran Lee: Yes! Bye for now, Misty!

Misty: Good bye for now, Bran Lee.

She hangs up the phone.

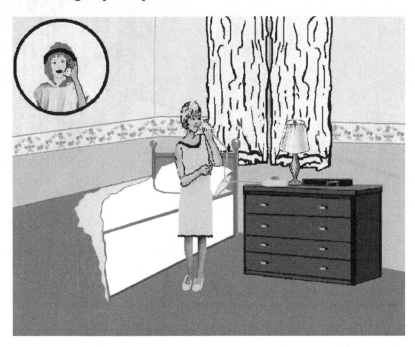

The next day, Bran Lee takes her cleaning
equipment down stairs to the Weatherton's
basement. She notices the book case on the
west wall of the basement.

She walks over to the book case and begins dusting. As she lifts the feather duster up to the books, she accidently hits the encyclopedia book initialed with the letter "D".

The wall opens.

Bran Lee: Oops ! Oh my!

Bran Lee walks into the secret room. She sees an open brief case in the corner. As she looks inside the brief case, she stares at a document inside. It's a Poem.

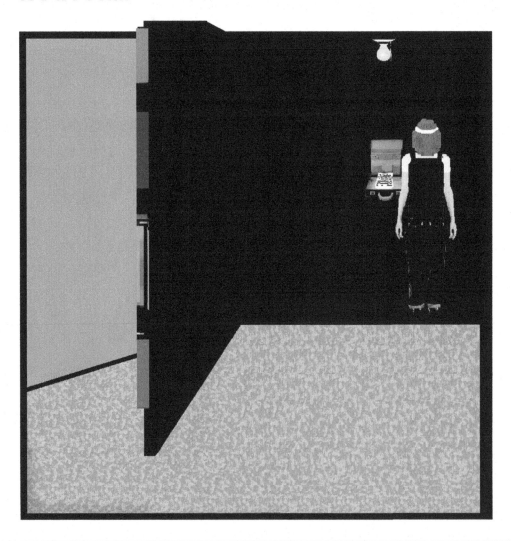

"FRAGILE"

IF I HAD A WISH...I'D WISH FOR A PLACE, WHERE I COULD SIT ALONE AND THINK OF YOUR FACE.

IF I HAD A THOUGHT, I'D DREAM OF A PEN THAT WOULD MAKE YOUR FACE BECOME VIVID AGAIN.

IF I HAD YOUR FACE PICTURED AT LAST,

YOUR PICTURED FACE WOULD TURN TO GLASS.

IF I HAD YOUR SMILE, NOTHING WOULD MATTER.

BUT IF YOU HAD TO FROWN....MY WHOLE WORLD WOULD SHATTER!

Bran Lee put the poem back into the brief case. She left the secret room, and finished her cleaning chores.

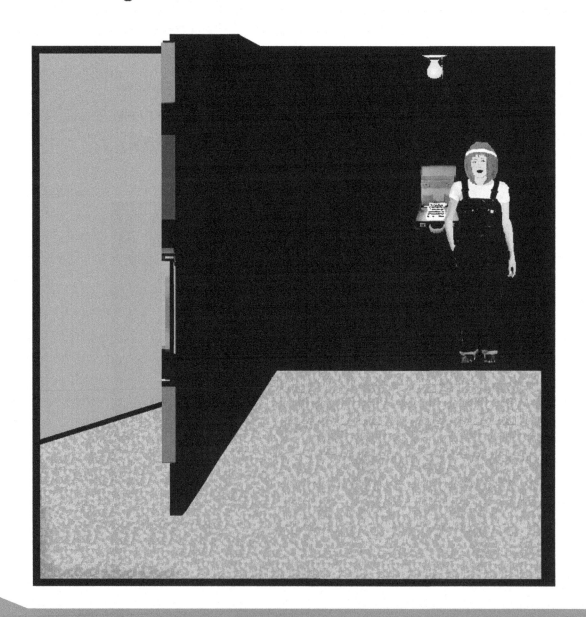

She went upstairs.

Meanwhile, Cassie calls Misty to let her know that the dishes have now come in.

Misty: Oh that is wonderful, Cassie! Thank you so much! And thank Roger, your computer, also! Nancia and I will be there to pick them up.

Misty, Nancia, and Bran Lee all have lunch at the Jolly Restaurant, after placing the dishes back in the box by the garage.

Nancia: So now that we have the dishes, how should we go about telling Mrs. Weatherton?

Misty: I think we should not tell her! If no harm has been done, then maybe Mrs. Weatherton never needs to know!

Bran Lee: But Misty, I wanted to tell you that I stumbled upon the secret room that you had told me about.

Nancia: You entered the secret room?

Bran Lee: Yes! And in the room was an open brief case with a poem inside.

Misty: A poem?

Bran Lee: A beautiful poem! I think we should confess to Mrs. Weatherton that we've replaced the dishes and that I found the poem!

Nancia: We could all tell her together!

The three girls enter the kitchen to speak with Mrs. Weatherton.

Bran Lee: Mrs. Weatherton, we have something that we want to tell you.

Mrs. Weatherton: Yes, what would that be dear?

Misty: I was driving my car and accidently ran over the box of dishes sitting in by the garage.

Nancia: It was an accident!

Misty: But we ordered the dishes from The Jolly Merchant, and we have replaced them!

Bran Lee: Everything is intact, just as it was before we broke them.

Mrs. Weatherton: Well....

Bran Lee: But I have a confession! When I was dusting the book case down stairs, I accidently stumbled upon your "secret room."

Mrs. Weatherton: But...

Bran Lee: I saw the poem that was in the brief case.

Mrs. Weatherton: Girls! Girls! I never had a box of dishes in the drive way! And I do not have a poem hidden in a brief case, in the secret room down stairs!

The girls look at each other.

Together: Then who would the dishes and the poem belong to?

Bran Lee: Mrs. Weatherton, has anyone else had access to the secret room before me?

Mrs. Weatherton: Well the girl who previously cleaned for us had access. She cleaned the book case down stairs often.

Misty: Who is she?

Mrs. Weatherton: Her name is Jitsu. She had to return to her home in Japan, which is the reason we hired you, Bran Lee.

Bran Lee: Well, I accidently stumbled upon the secret room, and I found the poem she had in the open brief case.

Misty: The set of dishes must also belong to her.

Nancia: We need to contact her to return the dishes, and the poem. I suppose the key to the safe deposit box is yours?

Mrs. Weatherton: Yes. I had the key in a special box. I suppose Jitsu placed the dishes in the box without knowing it. She was planning to be married to Katsu, the boy who lives down the street. But he changed his mind and Jitsu decided to return to Japan.

Bran Lee: Well I guess our work is finished for today.

Mrs. Weatherton: Thank you for replacing the dishes, girls. I will call Jitsu, and let her know that I will ship them to her.

Misty and Nancia say good bye, and leave.

Misty: (while driving in the car) I have a plan that may help Jitsu re-unite with Katsu.

Nancia: What do you have in mind?

Misty: Well, I noticed a sign at the library about a poetry contest. If we enter Jitsu's poem in the contest, then Katsu will see how much he means to her.

Nancia (Smiles) Bran Lee can get the poem for us. Let's enter it!

All of the girls are in front of the library reading the sign. Bran Lee is holding the poem.

—POETRY CONTEST—
SUBMISSIONS TAKEN AT THE FRONT DESK!

The next day, Misty is home in her kitchen, talking on the phone to Bran Lee.

Misty: They are going to reveal the winners of the poetry contest today! I can hardly wait!

Bran Lee: It will be very exciting if Jitsu wins the contest!

Misty: Meet me at the Library in one hour! I can't wait to see the look on Katsu's face if Jitsu wins!

Inside the library, the Contest host stands at the podium and reads the winner of this year's contest.

Host: The winner of this year's poetry contest is Jitsu Hakone's poem entitled "FRAGILE."

Katsu (approaches Bran Lee) I suppose you will be having Mrs. Weatherton contact Jitsu to tell her about the contest!

Bran Lee: Yes. I'm sure she will return from her home town to claim her winnings!

Nancia: Do you think she will be angry at us for submitting her work?

Misty: Of course not! Especially when she finds out that she won the 1st prize! Besides, Bran Lee stumbled upon it accidently.

Bran Lee: Isn't it exciting Katsu? Jitsu will return back to Jolly Town!

Katsu: (smiles) Please let me know, as soon as she arrives!

Jitsu has returned from Japan, and smiles at Katsu, while holding her trophy in Misty's kitchen.

Misty: I am so glad that you are moving back to Jolly Town, Jitsu!

Katsu: I have missed you very much!

Misty: I think we should all celebrate and go to THE JOLLY RESTAURANT! I'm buying everyone's dinner!

They all smile, and leave for the Jolly Restaurant.   The End

Printed in the United States
By Bookmasters